MySELF Bookshelf

Brown Bear's Dream

By YunYeong Kim

Illustrated by KyeMahn Kim

Language Arts Consultant: Joy Cowley

NORWOOD HOUSE PRESS

Chicago, Illinois

DEAR CAREGIVER   My**SELF** Bookshelf is a series of books that support children's social emotional learning. SEL has been proven to promote not only the development of self-awareness, responsibility, and positive relationships, but also academic achievement.

Current research reveals that the part of the brain that manages emotion is directly connected to the part of the brain that is used in cognitive tasks, such as: problem solving, logic, reasoning, and critical thinking—all of which are at the heart of learning.

SEL is also directly linked to what are referred to as 21st Century Skills: collaboration, communication, creativity, and critical thinking. MySELF Bookshelf offers an early start that will help children build the competencies for success in school and life.

In these delightful books, young children practice early reading skills while learning how to manage their own feelings and how to be considerate of other perspectives. Each book focuses on aspects of SEL that help children develop social competence that will benefit them in their relationships with others as well as in their school success. The charming characters in the stories model positive traits such as: responsibility, goal setting, determination, patience, and celebrating differences. At the end of each story, you will find a letter that highlights the positive traits and an activity or discussion to help your child apply SEL to his or her own life.

Above all, the most important part of the reading experience is to have fun and enjoy it!

Sincerely,

Shannon Cannon

Shannon Cannon, Ph.D.
Literacy and SEL Consultant

Norwood House Press • P.O. Box 316598 • Chicago, Illinois 60631
For more information about Norwood House Press please visit our website at www.norwoodhousepress.com or call 866-565-2900.

Shannon Cannon—Literacy and SEL Consultant
Joy Cowley—English Language Arts Consultant
Mary Lindeen—Consulting Editor

Library of Congress Cataloging-in-Publication Data
　　Kim, YunYeong.
　　 Brown Bear's dream / by YunYeong Kim ; illustrated by KyeMahn Kim.
　　　 pages cm. -- (Myself bookshelf)
　　 Summary: "Brown Bear dreams of seeing the sea. With the help of Grandpa Beaver, they set goals
and schedules so that Brown Bear can accomplish his dreams. Social and emotional learning concepts
include: setting goals, overcoming adversity, and being brave"-- Provided by publisher.
　　 ISBN 978-1-59953-646-0 (library edition : alk. paper) -- ISBN 978-1-60357-668-0 (ebook) [1.
Bears--Fiction. 2. Beavers--Fiction. 3. Swimming--Fiction. 4. Goal (Psychology)--Fiction. 5.
Perseverance (Ethics)--Fiction.] I. Kim, KyeMahn, illustrator. II. Title.
　　 PZ7.K562Br 2014
　　 [E]--dc23
　　　　　　　　　　　　　2014008792

Manufactured in the United States of America in Stevens Point, Wisconsin.
252N—072014

3

Spring came to the woods
and Brown Bear woke
from his winter sleep.
He wanted to climb a tree
to see the rest of the woods,
but that was impossible.
Brown Bear had hurt his leg
when it got caught in a trap.

Sitting on the riverbank,
Brown Bear watched the beavers.
How he wished that he could swim!
But that was also impossible
because of his leg.
He cried, "I want to swim
and be free and strong
like all those beavers."

Sometimes he tried to imitate
the beavers' movements.

Grandfather Beaver saw him
and said, "What are you doing?"

Brown Bear blushed.
"I'm practicing how to swim."

"Why are you doing that?"

Brown Bear said to him,
"I have this dream of going to the sea.
I can't walk there because I have a limp,
but I've heard that the river goes to the sea.
Maybe I can learn to swim."

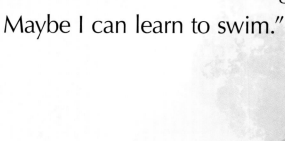

Grandfather Beaver wanted to help the bear.
"If you want to swim to the ocean,
I will go with you in the summer.
It will be March soon. Let's go in July."

They made goals for March, April, May, and June
and decided on what they would do.

The goal for Brown Bear in March
was to build up physical strength.
He did 100 push-ups on the ground.
He did 100 pull-ups on a tree branch.
He lifted 100 rocks every day.

The goal in April was to swim in the pond.
At first it was hard for Brown Bear to float,
but as the days passed, he learned to swim.

The goal in May was to swim in the river.
That was more difficult.
Brown Bear thought he might drown.

15

Exhausted, Brown Bear crawled
out of the river and said,
"I don't think I can do it."

"Nonsense!" said Grandfather Beaver.
"This is your dream! Keep working at it.
It is never easy to realize a dream.
If it was easy, it wouldn't be worth having."

That night, Brown Bear looked at the sky,
and he thought for a long, long time.

17

In June, Brown Bear practiced swimming
in the river. He also learned about the ocean.
He learned about big waves
and how to avoid dangerous creatures.

At last, it was July.
"Brown Bear, are you ready?"
asked Grandfather Beaver.

"Yes, I am ready," replied Brown Bear.

So Brown Bear and
Grandfather Beaver got
in the river and swam
with the current.

When the sun went down,
they slept on the riverbank.
When the sun rose,
they swam again.

The river grew wider.
That meant the sea was close.
But Grandfather Beaver said,
"Brown Bear, I am old
and my body is tired.
I can no longer go with you.
You must swim on by yourself."

22

Gathering courage,
Brown Bear swam on his own.

23

At last he came to the sea.
It was wider and more beautiful
than he had ever imagined.
"I did it! I did it!" he yelled.

Brown Bear went back home
and soon winter came.
He fell into a deep winter sleep.
Maybe he was dreaming up
a new dream.

Dear Brown Bear,

I know that it wasn't easy for you
to make your dream come true,
but you did it!
You got to the sea!
It was hard at first,
but you made goals
and kept working.
You asked for help.
You practiced.
You had courage.
I am so proud of you!

Your friend,
Grandfather Beaver

SOCIAL AND EMOTIONAL LEARNING FOCUS

Setting Goals and Overcoming Adversity

Brown Bear was able to achieve his dream of swimming to the sea because he set a goal and made a plan.

Think of something you would like to be able to do. On a sheet of paper write down what it would take for you to be able to do it. For example, Brown Bear needed to build physical strength before he could learn how to swim.

- Write down your goal.

- Write down 3 things you need to do to accomplish your goal.

- Next, create a calendar to plan how you will reach your goal. Think about the smaller goals and how much time you need to practice them so you can reach your main goal. If you put these goals on a calendar, including days and times you will practice, you can check them off as you work hard to reach your goal.

Monday	Tuesday	Wednesday	Thursday	Friday	Saturday	Sunday
1	2	3	4	5	6	7
8	9	10	11	12	13	14
15	16	17	18	19	20	21
22	23	24	25	26	27	28
29	30	1	2	3	4	5

Reader's Theater

Reader's Theater is an interactive approach to reading that allows students to understand each story through dramatic interpretation. By involving students in reading, listening, and speaking activities, they provide an integrated approach for students to develop fluency and comprehension. A Reader's Theater edition of this book is available online. You can access the script by scanning the QR code to the right or visit our website at: http://www.norwoodhousepress.com/brownbearsdream.aspx